# Even Villains Grant Wishes

LIANA BROOKS

# OTHER WORKS

## ALL I WANT FOR CHRISTMAS

All I Want For Christmas Is A Reaper
All I Want For Christmas Is A Werewolf

## FLEET OF MALIK

Bodies In Motion
Change of Momentum

## HEROES AND VILLAINS

Even Villains Fall In Love
Even Villains Go To The Movies
Even Villains Have Interns
Even Villains Play The Hero (books 1 – 3 omnibus)
The Polar Terror

## TIME AND SHADOWS

The Day Before
Convergence Point
Decoherence

## SHORTER WORKS

Fey Lights
Prime Sensations
Darkness and Good

Find other works by the author at
www.lianabrooks.com

# Even Villains Grant Wishes

INKLET #72

LIANA BROOKS

www.inkprintpress.com

Print ISBN: 978-1-922434-72-2
eBook ISBN: 9798201121815

www.inkprintpress.com

*National Library of Australia Cataloguing-in-Publication Data*
Brooks, Liana 1982 –
Even Villains Grant Wishes
52 p.
ISBN: 978-1-922434-72-2
Inkprint Press, Canberra, Australia
1. Fiction—Superheroes  2. Fiction—Short Stories

First Print Edition: December 2021
Cover photo © Anna_Om via Deposit Photos
Cover design © Inkprint Press
Interior art © Amy Laurens

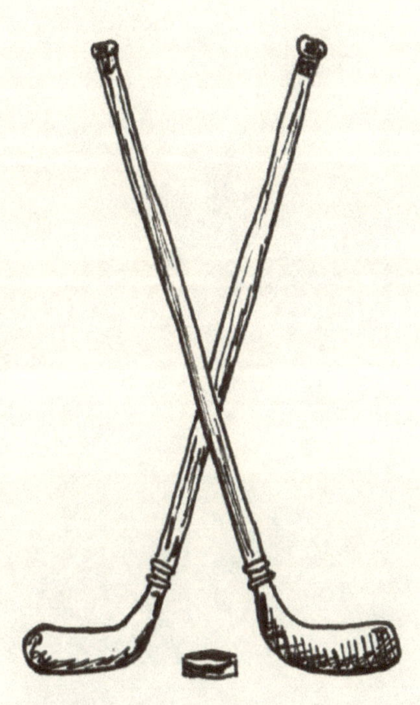

# EVEN VILLAINS GRANT WISHES

As a cold Yukon wind howled outside, Andrea scrolled through Tumblr—hashtag supervillains—looking for a cosplayer who would fit the bill. Her desktop computer screen was the only glow in the dark office where the scent of chamomile tea and candy canes lingered long after the holiday party had ended.

It was heartbreaking working with the Dreams Come True program at the pediatric hospital. Sure, it was wonderful when she could help the kids make a dream come true, but sometimes... sometimes it was all too much.

Everett Jones was a special one. His parents had been in a car wreck when he was four months old and an improperly fitted car seat had thrown him from the wreckage. It had saved his life—the semitruck behind their car hadn't been able to stop in time—but it had left Everett broken and orphaned. He'd been in and out of the foster care system until his aunt had graduated from college.

At seven, he should have been okay. But a little cold turned into bronchitis, and then they'd found abnormal growths along the tibia. And then the doctors at Merriton Pediatric Hospital, the premiere children's hospital in the Yukon Territory, found out that the donor from Everett's last surgery had not been screened correctly.

The bone cancer was sinking in.

Everett was seven and suicidal.

His adoptive mother was a wreck.

Andrea wanted to do nothing more than make sure Everett had one dream come true. She'd gone to his hospital room with binders, folders, and brochures.

Disneyland. Cruises. The Stanley Cup playoffs. She would make sure he got what he wanted.

And then Everett had asked for the absolutely impossible: a day with the Polar Terror, the only supervillain north of the 66th Parallel.

Andrea glanced at the clock. It was already two in the morning and she had her first meeting tomorrow at eight. Tanya Nothstien from the third floor (burn victims) was meeting with the Whitehorse Huskies and going to three days of hockey training camp, a reward for finally hitting her physical therapy milestone and being able to walk without braces. Tanya had a long road ahead, and at least one more surgery to repair her arm, but she could be a hockey goalie as she was.

The Huskies had even invited her to come play goalie at one of their home games once the season was in full swing.

In the afternoon, Andrea had to meet with the Jenwa family. Three-year-old Doug was terminal. Dreams Come True was getting the whole family together—grandmas and grandpas too—and flying them to Hawaii to celebrate what was expected to be Doug's last birthday.

Staring unthinkingly at the screen in front of her, Andrea grabbed a kleenex and wiped away the tears.

Tomorrow was going to be rough. She needed sleep. But...

Blurry-eyed, she hit the pencil icon on Tumblr and wrote a post.

*WANTED: The Polar Terror for a day of*

*fun and crime with 7yo Everett at the Merriton Pediatric Hospital.*

*Everett is a sweet boy who has had a bad run of luck. He wants to conquer the mountains with his favorite villain, and maybe rob a candy store.*

*If you're available, please email me at: andrea@canada.dreamcometrue.org*

She posted it with a sigh and turned the computer off. Yukon Territory was not a geek hub with ten thousand cosplayers. But, who knew? Maybe she'd get lucky and some rich American who could afford his own batmobile would feel like dressing up in traditional Yukon furs and flying up here.

The next day didn't dawn so much as slink in well after Andrea was at work. Winter mornings up here were an illusion more than a reality.

By ten, the hospital was sending home non-essential staff because of an incoming blizzard. Andrea shut her door, turned off the overhead light, and worked by the light of the street-light. No one could send her home if they didn't know she was there.

Lunch was a bag of pretzels nabbed from the vending machine while the hospital director dealt with a car collision in the parking garage. And at two, she went up to see Doug's family.

His room was filled with red toy robots, red balloons, and a red stuffed dog that was bigger than he was. Andrea confirmed all the details, checked with Dr. Harper to ensure that Doug was up for travel, checked with Doug's nursing staff to make sure all their paperwork was in order, and—worn out and ready to cry—limped back to her office.

It was cold.

Bone-freezing cold.

Andrea was Yukon born and bred, but negative 10 Celsius with snow swirling around her desk as she opened the door was too much. Her lips puckered as she sucked in a sob.

Someone—some utter bastard—had broken her window.

She closed her office door quietly behind her. There was no need to be rude, she told herself. There was cardboard behind the filing cabinet and the Good Lord had given her duct tape and common sense, more than enough to fix anything, as her grand-mère had always said.

Andrea turned to reach for the down coat hanging on the back of her door and screamed.

There was a person standing there.

A huge, fur-covered aberration with a spear in one hand and a rabbit-fur pouch at his hip. All the emotions of the day came pouring out in an ear-piercing wail that was swallowed by the howling wind outside. The bowl of tiny, polished rocks on her desk jumped and rattled as the wind stormed through the office, confining her, trapping her.

Terror squeezed her lungs. Fear climbed her spine with icy picks.

Death seemed only a breath away.

And then it finally stopped; her throat was swelling and scratching like she'd screamed for hours. Maybe she had and simply hadn't noticed over the bone-deep dread.

The snow stopped swirling and the stranger flicked their wrist. The wind rose and slammed the window shut.

"Sorry about the entrance?" the menace offered.

Andrea stalked behind her flimsy wooden desk, sat down in her creaking, broken chair in a huff, and grabbed a kleenex. Then a throat lozenge. She glared at the face hidden by a black balaclava.

"You, um, asked for me on Tumblr." The voice was deep. Definitely masculine. Almost apologetic.

She opened the bottom drawer of her desk and pulled out a fresh bottle of water. It was against her policy to drink bottled water unless the pipes froze, but this was an emergency. Sometimes her carbon footprint had to take a back seat to panic.

The person shuffled and took a seat in the stiff-backed client chair.

After several minutes, and half a bottle of water, Andrea sighed. "All right. That didn't go well. I try not to scream at anyone." She glanced at the window. "Who are you? And why is there snow melting on my desk?"

"It can't stay snow in this heat."

Andrea glared. "What I meant is; why didn't you come through the front door? We have a receptionist."

"They went home early. A security guard told me everyone had, so I came up here to leave a note."

"Through my window."

The masked face turned to consider the now-unbroken glass. "Eh... It made sense at the time?" He lifted his shoulder and dropped it. There was a slight twang in his voice. Almost...

"Are you from Newfoundland?"

He turned faster than she expected. "How'd you—"

"It's the accent. I dated a guy from there once. It didn't end well." Andrea realized her hand had tightened around her limited-edition Glamdring letter opener, and dropped it.

She wasn't going to risk getting blood on a collectible. At least, not a limited-edition one.

She had a Toronto Maple Leafs hockey stick, signed by Leo Komarov. She could part with that.

"You did want to see me, didn't you?" With gloved hands, the man reached into his rabbit-skin pouch and pulled out a folded piece of paper that he held out for her.

Andrea stood just enough to reach out and take the paper between her pointer and middle finger, then plopped back down. Glaring at him, she unfolded it with great ceremony. It was a screen capture of her desperate Tumblr post.

She shut her eyes.

This was the problem with the geek community: when cosplayers got into something, they really went all out. She was willing to bet that later— much later—when she wasn't so worn out, she'd find the string this guy had used to tug the window closed so it looked like he was using the wind.

"You don't look happy," the man said. "I thought, children's hospital and all, it might be time sensitive. And I was in town."

"Of course." Andrea closed her eyes and rubbed the bridge of her nose. "I'm sorry. I've had a very... rough... afternoon. I was expecting an email. There's paperwork to be done. If you cosplay for a living, you can use your time as a tax write-off. We also have security checks and things like that."

"I won't pass those," he said. "I'm a supervillain. An ecoterrorist or a planet defender, depends on who you ask."

Andrea opened one eye to glare at him. "I appreciate your dedication to the role, mister...?" She held out her hand as invitation for him to fill in the blank.

"Terror. Polar Terror." The way he pronounced it rhymed with 'bear'.

She looked at her water bottle and willed it to become a Chilkoot Larger from Yukon Brewing Co. The color didn't blush the deep amber of ripening wheat, so she figured she still hadn't come up with the ability to spontaneously make alcohol appear. Pity.

"Do you want colder water?" the man asked.

"No. I want beer, but I can't have it during working hours and I usually only drink on my birthday, Canada Day, and New Year's Eve. This is not a job where I need more depressants in my life."

"I thought bringing good cheer to kids would make for happy work."

Her sour smile was enough to make him lean back. "It's great when you actually can help. Some of our kids will recover. But they don't all walk out of here healthy and alive." She shrugged with one shoulder. "This afternoon I had to talk to a family whose little boy probably won't live to see four."

"Oh." His head tilted to the floor. "Is that Everett?"

"No. Everett is seven, he was in a car accident and had several surgeries to fix broken bones. One of the bone grafts left him with bone cancer."

There was a moment of silence, a place for grief.

"His parents must be devastated," the man said, quietly.

"They're dead." Andrea hated how callous she sounded, but she was out of emotion. "His aunt has custody. She's a very nice woman, but totally overwhelmed. Her sister, Everett's mother, was the only family she had. She's been working hard to raise Everett and be supportive through everything, but she really doesn't have anyone else to lean on." Andrea picked up Glamdring and spun the miniature sword around. "They have your comic books."

The man nodded. "All the proceeds go to college funds for kids from the Yukon Territory, you know. I don't get paid for that. I didn't license it either, but..."

He shrugged, and Andrea thought she heard a hint of a smile when he said, "I had a word with the duo drawing the comics and we worked things out."

"They donate all the money, and you don't kill them with your freeze-ray?"

"See, the way you say it sounds so mean. And it's not a freeze-ray. That's something only fake supervillains need. I have superpowers."

"Uh-huh. Because you were born under the northern lights during an eclipse on the winter solstice, but your mom went into labor early and couldn't get out of her house, and she died of blood loss. I read the comic."

"They left out the part where she only couldn't leave the house because her car had been repossessed because she lost her job when an oil company bought the resort she worked for and tore it down, along with two hundred acres of virgin forest. She couldn't pay to heat the house. She was freezing, went into labor, had me, and died."

Andrea narrowed her eyes. "I read the comic."

"I lived it."

She rolled her eyes. "Of course."

He reached out a gloved hand and the puddles of melted snow on her desk froze and cracked. The water in her bottle froze. Her hands turned blue with cold.

"Holy guacamole!" Andrea jumped out of her chair, teeth chattering, and grabbed the signed hockey stick.

The temperature rose. Slightly.

"Are you going to challenge me to a game?"

"I'm going to beat you with it."

He tilted his head.

"It's this or I stab you with my letter opener, but that's a limited-edition

Hobbit Glamdring from the WETA Workshops."

"I guess I know where I rate."

"The hockey stick is signed."

"St. John's Ice Caps?"

"Maple Leafs."

He shook his head. "You ought to burn it. You really should. I'll get you something from a good hockey team."

Knuckles rapped on her office door. "Andrea, are you still here?" It was Dr. Kobbler, the head of research and the hospital's unofficial boss. Kandi Stevens, the actual hospital chief administrator, only came in if there was a funding emergency. She made sure the doors stayed open, kids got what they needed, and that no politicians got in the way of finding cures, and then she left the actual medical teams to handle the rest.

"I'm here, Dr. Kobbler." She glared at the Polar Terror. "Sit down," she whispered, "and behave. Or it's the Maple Leafs for you!"

"You're Canadian," he grumbled. "Pretend to be nice."

She stuck out her tongue as the door opened, then turned with a happy smile. "Dr. Kobbler, I didn't know you were still here."

"Still here." He looked around the room through his gold-rimmed glasses and frowned in confusion. "Are you not getting enough heat in here? I can call Ms. Stevens."

"It's fine."

Dr. Kobbler looked at the Polar Terror, took off his glasses and methodically cleaned them, and then looked again. "Nope. Still there. Is this one of your...?" He waved his hand in a vague gesture.

"Yes, this is—" She cut herself off.

"Kodiak Old Crow."

Andrea bit her tongue. It was possibly a real name. There were plenty of

First Nations people in the Yukon, but Old Crow was also a town at the far north end of the territory that was, at least in the comics, where the Polar Terror went to grade school.

"Well, Mr. Old Crow, it's wonderful that you've come out to help the children. Bit of a bad day for it. The weather's taken a turn for the worst," Dr. Kobbler said. "Andrea." He gave her a significant look. "You were supposed to go home this morning."

"It's my fault," the Terror said quickly. "She couldn't reach me to cancel our appointment. So she stayed. To be polite."

Dr. Kobbler nodded. "Of course. Andrea, you are a wonder, but I think I should send you south for six months or so. Sometimes you need American rudeness. This would have been the kind of day where leaving early and missing an appointment would be acceptable. Rude, and terribly American, but acceptable."

"Of course, Dr. Kobbler. But I do live within walking distance of the hospital, and I have my snow shoes. I'll be fine."

"So, this is our, um, Polar Terror?" Dr. Kobbler asked. "The costume looks very authentic."

"It is authentic," the Terror grumbled.

Andrea let her hockey stick go and crossed her arms. "He's interested in cosplaying the Polar Terror for one of our superhero days. And, Everett wants to go rob a candy store with him."

"I was going to ask about that," the Terror said. "There's no good candy stores near here. I checked. And I usually don't steal things. I stop the destruction of natural resources."

"And freeze people to death," she couldn't help but point out.

"Only if they really deserve it."

She rolled her eyes.

Dr. Kobbler clapped. "Oh, wonderful job, Andrea! He sounds just like the comic book hero."

"Super villain," Andrea and the Terror corrected in unison.

"Of course," Dr. Kobbler said in the fake-serious voice he used with very earnest children who wanted to lecture an adult on the care of their stuffed animals.

Dr. Kobbler's late wife had been an actress in her younger years, and she'd left all her money to the hospital to build a mini-wing just for the care of dolls, stuffed animals, and other beloved Lovies who needed expert care. Long term patients were given access as their health permitted, and lab coats so they could practice their medical skills. Dr. Kobbler had always made a point to stop by the Gracie Wing several times a day to consult with the young 'doctors' there.

It was one of the more endearing facets of working at Merriton Pediatric.

Even on the worst days, Andrea knew the whole hospital was working to make the kids feel like healthy, happy, normal kids. And the whole community of Merriton was behind them. From the custom doll-maker who painted action figures and dollies to look like their kids, to the pastry chef who made special gluten-soy-nut-free cakes full of vegetables but still tasting of chocolate, to the actors who put on shows, to the high school students who came down every Wednesday to read aloud, to the retirees who came to play games with the patients... Everyone was here for the kids who flew in from all over the Yukon, and sometimes even from the bush of Alaska.

With a reluctant sigh, Andrea put on a brave face. "We should—"

"—go up?" Dr. Kobbler suggested. "What a wonderful idea! I noticed that Everett didn't go to the Gracie Wing today, even though he has a toy in there. And Kaddy's car is still here. She'll probably be spending the night again."

That wasn't at all what Andrea wanted to suggest.

Taking an unvetted mad man who could freeze anything up to the hospital floor to visit Everett was not within her comfort zone. But it would make Everett happy to see his hero. She teetered between the need to see Everett smile and the fierce instinct to protect the kids she played fairy godmother for.

"You look worried," the Terror said.

"Super villain, hospital... Real fur..."

"It's clean!" he protested. "I promise, I'm not sick and won't be a threat to the kids."

"The problem with that promise is that you are a super villain. I can't trust you."

The Polar Terror heaved a dramatic sigh. "What would make you trust me?"

Andrea looked at Dr. Kobbler, who was watching them with the bemused but slightly absent smile of someone watching a junior champion's tennis match. No help there. Frustrated, she searched for inspiration.

Suddenly, it hit her. She opened her desk and pulled out two still-sealed copies of the Polar Terror comics she'd ordered for Everett a month ago. Then she put Glamdring on the stack. "Place your right hand on the comics and the left hand up, please."

The Polar Terror complied.

"Repeat after me: I, state your name, swear on the trust of my fandom and the group-think of Tumblr that I will not use my powers for evil while in this hospital."

"I, the Polar Terror, swear on the trust of my fandom and the group-think of Tumblr that I will not use my powers for evil while in this hospital."

Andrea went on, "If I endanger anyone here, or use my powers for evil, I will publicly admit I am a weenie and forever forswear both Tumblr and Reddit, so help me Gandalf."

"If I endanger anyone here, or use my powers for evil, I will publicly admit I am a weenie and forever forswear both Tumblr and Reddit, so help me Gandalf, Granny Weatherwax, and Professor Xavier."

"Ooo!" Dr. Kobbler murmured. "Reaching for the Discworld books. Very daring. I approve."

Pratchett's cantankerous old witch probably wouldn't, but she'd approve of the headology Andrea was using, so maybe it would shake out in the end.

Andrea tugged the improvised geek bible back. "Very well. Remember, the stake of your Tumblr account and your future as a non-weenie is at stake here."

"I will uphold this most solemn oath," he promised. Then he turned to Dr. Kobbler and stage-whispered, "She threatened to beat me with a hockey stick earlier."

The doctor turned with a raised eyebrow. "The Maple Leafs one?"

Andrea nodded.

"I like the Maple Leafs!" Dr. Kobbler protested. "Really, Andrea, remind me to get you a whaling spear next time I go to a conference in Alaska. I can't believe you'd use a hockey stick," he muttered. "That's practically blasphemy."

She shrugged. "Considering the game, I thought a little blood would make it look more authentic."

"I never got into fights when I played hockey," Dr. Kobbler protested as he held the door open and ushered them towards the elevators. "I was voted Most Congenial in my junior league when I was six."

"That's probably why you went into pediatric medicine instead of the NHL," Andrea said as she punched the button to call the elevator.

The Polar Terror looked around. "It's kind of quiet in here."

"Most of the staff went home," Dr. Kobbler said. "This storm blew in out of nowhere."

The Terror shuffled a little. "Um, do you want it to stop?"

"Oh!" Dr. Kobbler chuckled and winked. "Right! Yes, please, Mr. Polar Terror, sir! Stop this awful storm!" He elbowed the Terror with a laugh. "You're such a hoot. The kids are going to eat this up."

Andrea glanced out the window as they stepped into the elevator. She had a cold certainty that the storm would end very quickly. She might live to regret this…

But at least little Everett's dream would come true.

# THE MAKING OF *EVEN VILLAINS GRANT WISHES*

This story (and, in fact, the whole *The Polar Terror* book) are all Tumblr's fault.

There I was, mindlessly scrolling through fandom memes and GIFs and Tumblr throws a story prompt at me.

It was a wicked little idea. A super villain showing up at a hospital and being mistaken as a cosplayer. The poor Make-A-Wish coordinator dealing with volunteering villains.

I meant to make it a little short story and it grew and all of a sudden I had a whole book: *The Polar Terror. Even Villains Grant Wishes* was originally the opening. It didn't quite fit, but it's found new life here as an Inklet.

# Read more by Liana Brooks!

# THE POLAR TERROR
## *CHAPTER ONE*

Kaddy leaned her head against the pale yellow wall of the hospital room, closed her eyes, and tried not to hear the constant whooshing and beeping of the machines.

The ticky-tick-tick of the heartrate monitor.

The two-minute beep as the IV dropped another controlled dose of pain medications that seemed to do no good.

The whock-whock-whock of the second hand on the clock.

There was no escape.

She couldn't even run outside to the snow and let that peace envelope her. Not while Everett was lying in bed, staring out the window at the flat roof of the parking garage, refusing to talk.

With a sigh, she tried to reach him. Again. "Do you want to watch some TV?"

Everett didn't move.

"We could play with your action figures." She pushed herself out of the uncomfortable chair and walked over to his bed.

Everett let her pull the plush Polar Terror doll out of his listless hand.

She bopped him on the nose with it. "The Polar Terror is coming! He'll walk right out of this storm and—"

Everett rolled to the side, crossing his tiny arms as best he could. His bottom lip quavered with anger and pain.

"I'm sorry." Kaddy put the doll back next to him. "We're going to find a way through this, Ev. I promise. And then we'll sew you the Polar Terror costume you wanted."

"There is no Polar Terror," Everett whispered, his first words all day. "Nobody comes to rescue you."

She rubbed his shoulder gently. "I know, bud. That's why you have me. You and me, we can handle anything."

"Not this," he whispered. "Not cancer."

Tears choked her. "We will," she whispered just as a softly. "We'll find a way to make it all right."

Everett squeezed his eyes shut.

Kaddy slumped back. Even if—and it was a really big if—the hospital pulled off a miracle and Everett got better, she wasn't going back to a job.

Her firm had been very patient, let her take a leave of absence, but her boss was retiring and the incoming boss hadn't liked her. He'd questioned her education, her field time, her work ethic... And while the guy couldn't come out and say it, his tone all but screamed SINGLE MOMS NEED NOT APPLY.

She shook her head. Being a single

mom hadn't been her choice. She wasn't even dating when Everett was born.

But then there'd been a car accident a semester before graduation. Her sister and brother-in-law were killed on impact.

The idea of being a working, single parent was terrifying, but letting Everett bounce between foster families wasn't an option either.

Squeezing the guard rail of his hospital bed, she stood up. One way or another, she'd make a good life for him. That's what moms did.

There was a tentative knock at the door, like the person on the other side was hoping they wouldn't get an answer, but knew they would.

Rolling her eyes, Kaddy cracked it open for the inevitable nurse.

Andrea, the ever-perky Dream Co-ordinator for Merriton Pediatric Hospital, looked at her with the world's fakest smile, wide, frightened blue eyes, and damp blonde hair that looked like she'd gone outside without her usual hat.

"Yessssss?" Kaddy dragged the word out.

Andrea squeezed through the tiny crack in the doorway and slammed the door shut. "Okay. Hi, Kaddy! Everett! It is so good to see you two!" The words were rushed, panicked, and had the forced joviality of true terror.

But this was the Yukon in mid-winter, not some American city where a bomber was going to hold them hostage. "Is… is everything okay?" Kaddy asked.

The only thing that would scare Andrea was a really bad diagnosis. Kaddy's stomach flipped as tears welled up in her eyes.

She couldn't handle that.

"Just dandy!" Andrea's voice squeaked. "Actually." She faked a laugh.

"Funny story. Everett has a visitor. And, I know he's been so tuckered out, the poor thing, so I was thinking we should reschedule. Don't you? That's great!" she rushed on, not letting Kaddy answer. "I'll cancel. He can come back some other time."

Not bad news then.

Everett rolled over in his bed, forehead wrinkled in confusion.

"Who came?" Kaddy asked. The hospital attracted an eclectic group of visitors. Usually hockey stars, medical students, and politicians on goodwill tours.

But Andrea welcomed all of them with open arms. "It isn't the Maple Leafs again, is it?"

No one this far north loved the Maple Leafs.

Andrea's head shook so hard Kaddy worried the woman was going to give herself a concussion.

"Okay..." Kaddy glanced over at Everett, who was showing the first interest in anything since his chemo treatment two days earlier. "Is there a reason you don't want this person to see Everett?" She licked her lips and mouthed, *Is it child services?*

"Worse," Andrea whispered hoarsely. She leaned forward and murmured a name in Kaddy's ear.

Kaddy's eyebrows went up in surprise. "Like... for real? You—" She stopped herself just in time and leaned forward. "You found a cosplayer to play the Polar Terror?"

She couldn't keep the excitement out of her whisper. Everett was going to be over the moon.

"No." Andrea shook her head and glanced over her shoulder. The color drained from her face. "He's... he's not fake."

"Who isn't fake?" Everett demanded from the bed.

"Just say no." Andrea grabbed Kaddy's elbow. "Please?"

Kaddy shook the other woman off and looked at the door. There was a thin layer of frost on the door. A suspiciously thin layer. Like someone was intentionally cooling the door for a grand entrance.

She narrowed her eyes.

Would the Dream Coordinator come in here acting terrified just to sell the idea of a super villain at the hospital? Yes. Yes she would.

It's exactly the sort of thing a perky, cheerful-before-coffee, former cheerleader would do.

Kaddy crossed her arms and sighed dramatically. "I don't know, Andrea. Ev's had a really rough week. I don't think he should have visitors. Not even the Polar Terror."

The heartrate monitor screamed in excitement as Everett sat up like he was attached to a spring. "The Polar Terror?"

With a burst of cold air, the door fell inward. Ice crystals glittered as icicles formed on the ceiling.

That was some impressive special effects budget.

A man in the Polar Terror's costume stepped in, towering over even Kaddy, who hadn't been called short since she turned thirteen and shot up. The muskrat parka, a rabbit fur hat, a strip of seal skin, a fur pouch, beadwork on his boots... and of course the very modern black balaclava with the Under Armor logo.

The Polar Terror had come to Merriton.

Keep reading! Head to
www.inkprintpress.com/
lianabrooks/heroesandvillains/
polarterror/
to buy your copy now!

# ABOUT THE AUTHOR

LIANA BROOKS loves hot summer days, sandy beaches, and being as close to the equator at sea level as possible. Which explains why she felt quite flummoxed when life led her to a house in the mountains outside Anchorage, Alaska. It was cold. It was snowy. It had moose and bears. And the beaches were rocky.

During the summers Alaska is breathtaking, but Liana found herself snowed in more than once and, with nothing better to do when curled by a fire sipping hot cocoa, she decided to write about an Arctic superhero. She thinks the story turned out rather well.

If you enjoyed the book too you can read more from Liana, from fantasy to sci-fi, on her website at:
www.LianaBrooks.com

#### INKLETS

Collect them all! Released on the 1st and 15th
of each month.

INKLET #055
Allure
AMY LAURENS

INKLET #056
The LIES We KNOW
LIANA BROOKS


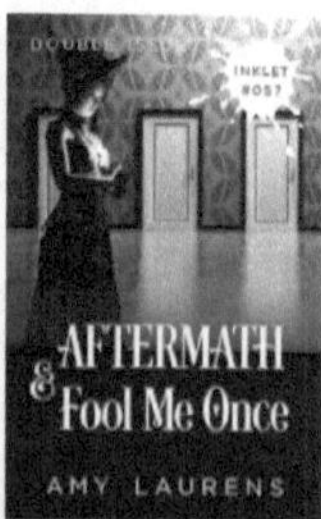

DOUBLE
INKLET #057
AFTERMATH & Fool Me Once
AMY LAURENS

INKLET #058
Purity
An Age Of Unicorns Story
AMY LAURENS

INKLET #059
Saved
AMY LAURENS

INKLET #060
A Kiss is the Secret
AMY LAURENS

INKLET #061
A Changing Tides Story
Fire Bright
AMY LAURENS

INKLET #062
Hades AND Persephone
LIANA BROOKS

INKLET #063
Just So Long As You're Happy
AMY LAURENS

INKLET #064
Theft Of A Lifetime
LIANA BROOKS

INKLET #065
Shoe
AMY LAURENS

INKLET #066
Published AUTHOR
LIANA BROOKS

DOUBLE ISSUE
INKLET #067
THE REMARKABLE INSIGHT OF JELLYBEANS & Understanding
AMY LAURENS

INKLET #068
Desperate Measures
AMY LAURENS

INKLET #069
Rock-a-bye
LIANA BROOKS

INKLET #070
the Other Carly
AMY LAURENS

INKLET #071
By Bioluminescent Light
AMY LAURENS

INKLET #072
Even Villains Grant Wishes
A Heroes & Villains Story
LIANA BROOKS